I0754838

TEACHING *for* CHANGE

How Septima Clark Led the Civil Rights Movement to Voting Justice

TEACHING for CHANGE

How Septima Clark Led the Civil Rights Movement to Voting Justice

Written by Yvonne Clark-Rhines *with* Monica Clark-Robinson

Illustrated by Abigail Albano-Payton

Quill Tree Books
An Imprint of HarperCollinsPublishers

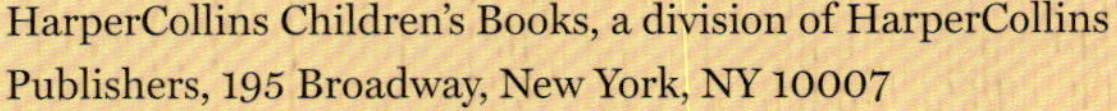

HarperCollins Children's Books, a division of HarperCollins Publishers, 195 Broadway, New York, NY 10007

HarperCollins Publishers, Macken House, 39/40 Mayor Street Upper, Dublin 1, D01 C9W8, Ireland

Quill Tree Books is an imprint of HarperCollins Publishers.

Teaching for Change: How Septima Clark Led the Civil Rights Movement to Voting Justice

Library of Congress Control Number: 2025937156
ISBN 978-0-06-325160-1

The artist used oil on canvas to create the illustrations for this book.
25 26 27 28 29 RTLO 10 9 8 7 6 5 4 3 2 1
First Edition

To my mother, who gave me life and the courage to follow my dreams.
And to my grandmother, who raised me with endless love
and gave me a wonderful life filled with joy and wisdom.

Mama Seppie, your strength and care have shaped me
into who I am today.

With all my love and gratitude,

—Y.C.R.

For Yvonne, whose friendship is so very dear to me.
It's been one of the greatest honors of my life to work with you.

And, of course, for Septima—may she rest in power.
You inspire me every single day.

—M.C.R.

For my parents—thank you for believing in my creativity,
even when I couldn't see where it would lead.
Your unwavering support made this possible.

—A.A.P.

Septima Clark was:
Born poor.
Born Black.
Born a girl.

It was hard to be even *one* of those things when she was born in 1898.

Her daddy had been enslaved at birth, bound by an unjust system.
Her mama had been raised free in Haiti, proud servant to none.

They wanted more for their daughter
than they saw in the world around them,
more than the white world wanted her to have.
And they believed that getting an education was the key.

When Septima was six, she attended school, but it wasn't much.
Black students had to sit
all day, every day,
on the bleachers, doing nothing.

So Septima's mother made a trade with a former teacher who lived nearby: clean laundry and babysitting in exchange for a *real* education for her daughter.

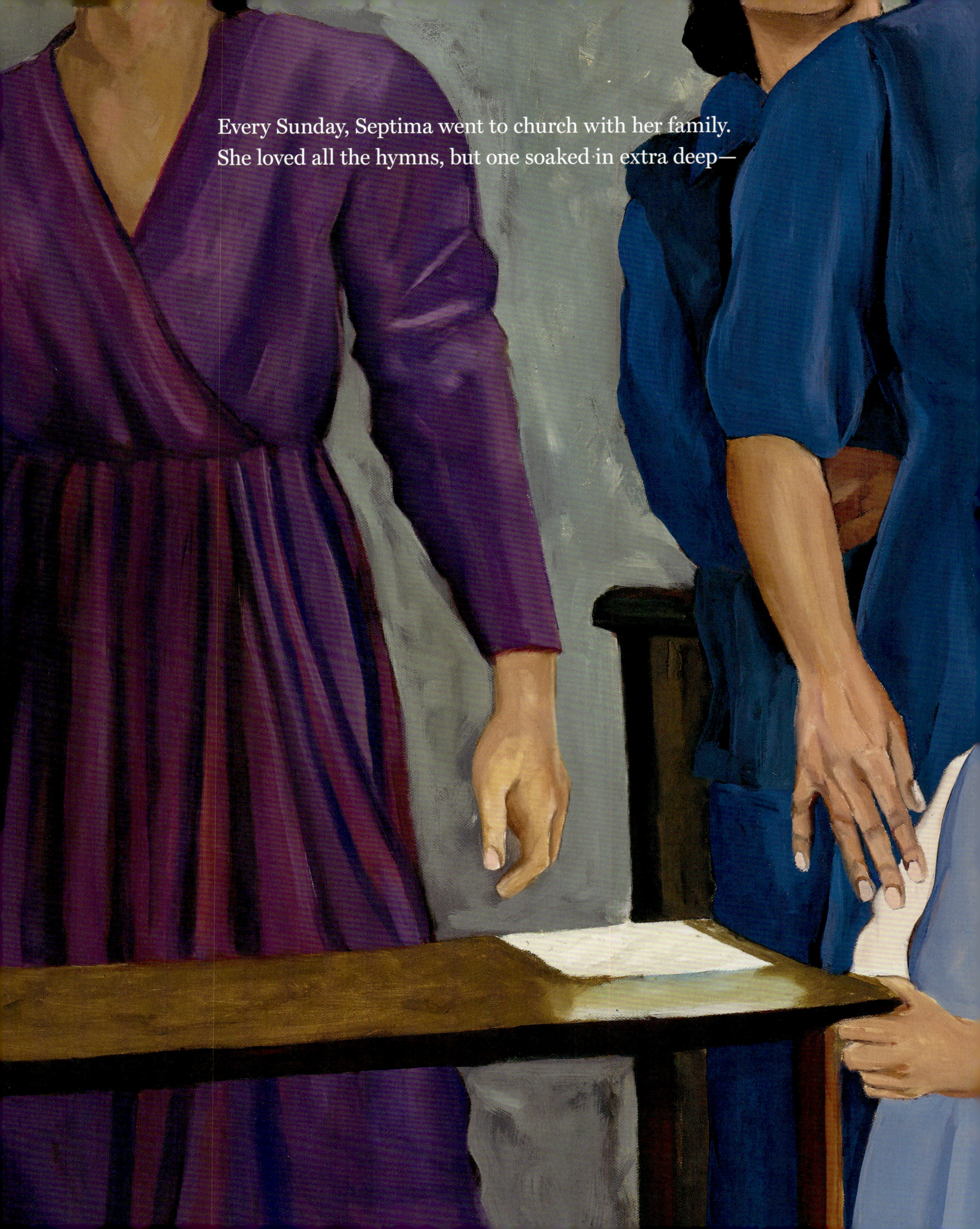

Every Sunday, Septima went to church with her family.
She loved all the hymns, but one soaked in extra deep—

Ain't gonna let nobody turn me 'round,
turn me 'round, turn me 'round,
I'm gonna keep on a-walkin',

keep on a-talkin',

marchin' up to freedom land.

Septima was a teacher even as a child—
"Little Ma," folks in the neighborhood called her.
She would teach anyone who would listen,
and children would gather around to learn.

Even though every card she'd been dealt
was stacked against her,
from a young age, there was a fire in Septima.
Her daddy taught her peace
and her mama taught her strength—
and with those as her guide,
Septima could *always* find a way.

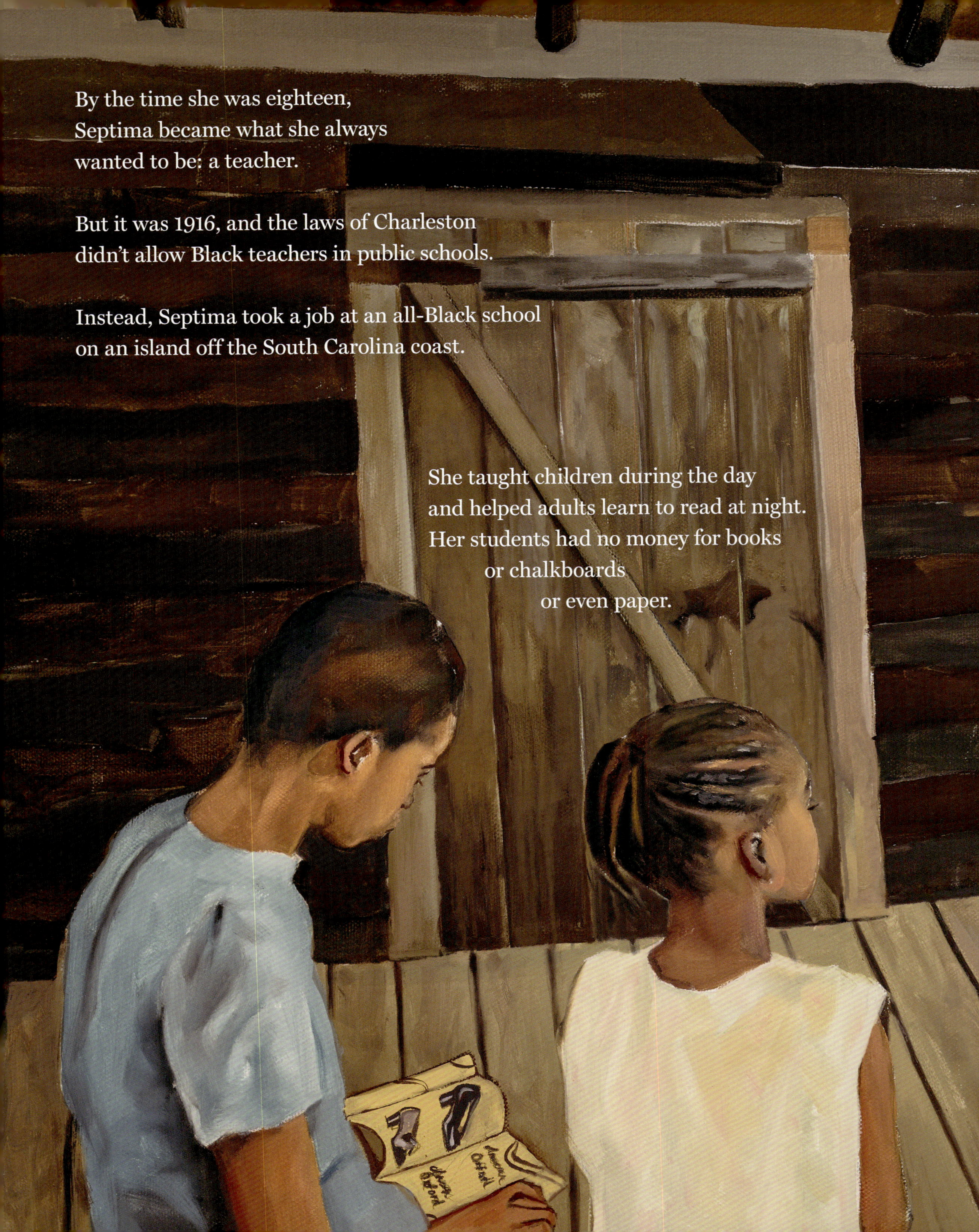

By the time she was eighteen,
Septima became what she always
wanted to be: a teacher.

But it was 1916, and the laws of Charleston
didn't allow Black teachers in public schools.

Instead, Septima took a job at an all-Black school
on an island off the South Carolina coast.

She taught children during the day
and helped adults learn to read at night.
Her students had no money for books
or chalkboards
or even paper.

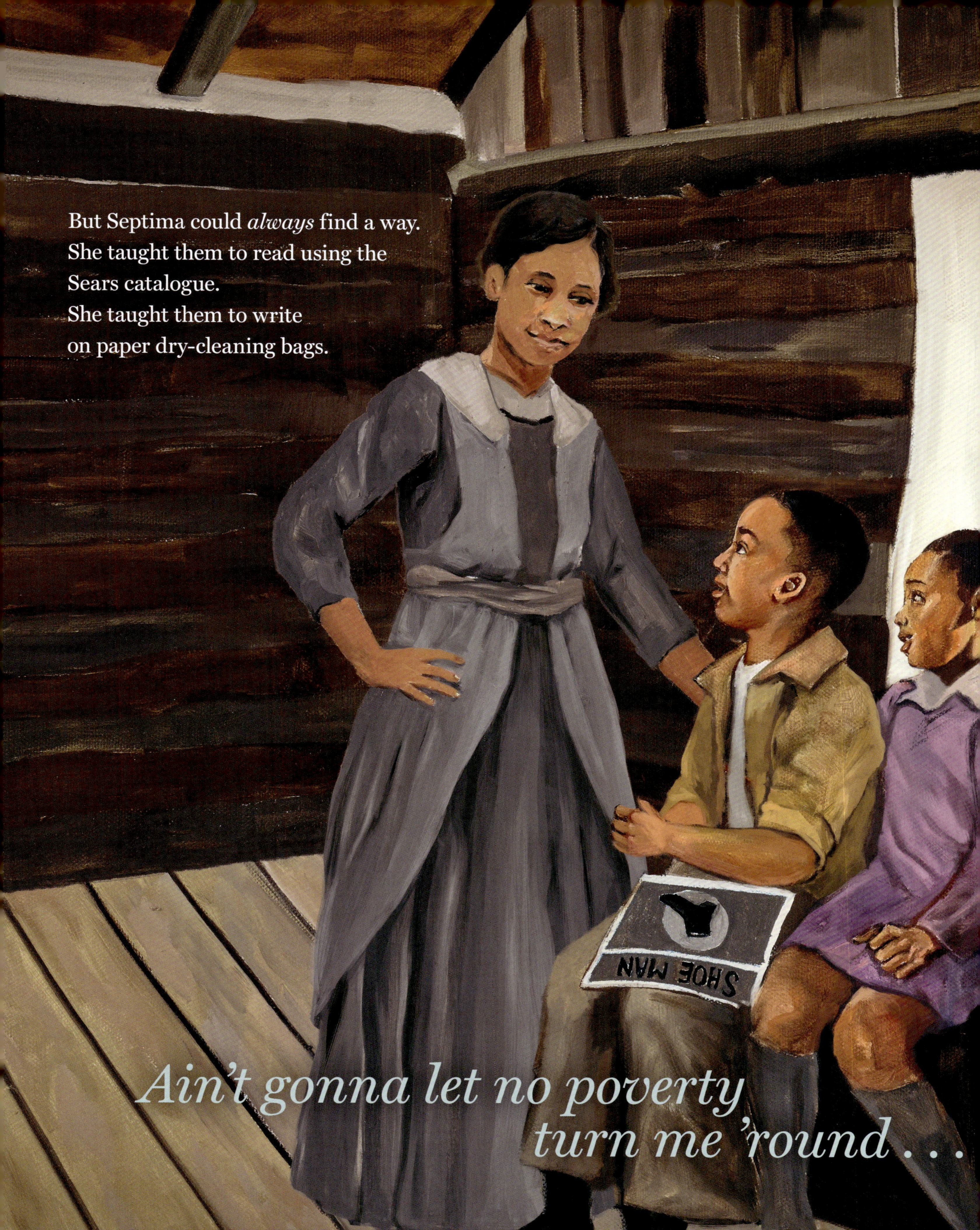

But Septima could *always* find a way.
She taught them to read using the
Sears catalogue.
She taught them to write
on paper dry-cleaning bags.

*Ain't gonna let no poverty
turn me 'round . . .*

In the 1950s, Black citizens in the South had to take tests to vote, tests that white people didn't have to take.

Many Black men and women hadn't been taught to read and write, so very few Black residents in the South could exercise their right to vote.

The politicians knew that voting was power, and they wanted to keep Black citizens far from it.

But Septima wouldn't stand for it.
It was a cruel and unjust plan,
and she knew, bone-deep, that it wasn't right.
Her education gave her a voice where others had none,
and Septima believed she had a responsibility
as a teacher to help others have a voice too.

She saw and felt discrimination everywhere in the South, and decided to do everything in her power to fight it.

Septima believed that *all* people—
Poor people
Black people
Female people—
deserved a fair shot, same as everyone.

Ain't gonna let
racism
turn me 'round . . .

She took a new job at an integrated school for adults in Tennessee.
There, she held classes about racial justice and peaceful activism
and established "citizenship schools,"
teaching folks to own their rights
so they could right the wrongs.

"Literacy means liberation!" she taught.

When students left Septima's class,
they knew how:

to read and write
to pass the voting tests
to be leaders and activists
in their own communities.

More than anything, they knew
how to *be the change.*

Septima's students were from many races, creeds, and religions—
all people were welcome in her classes.

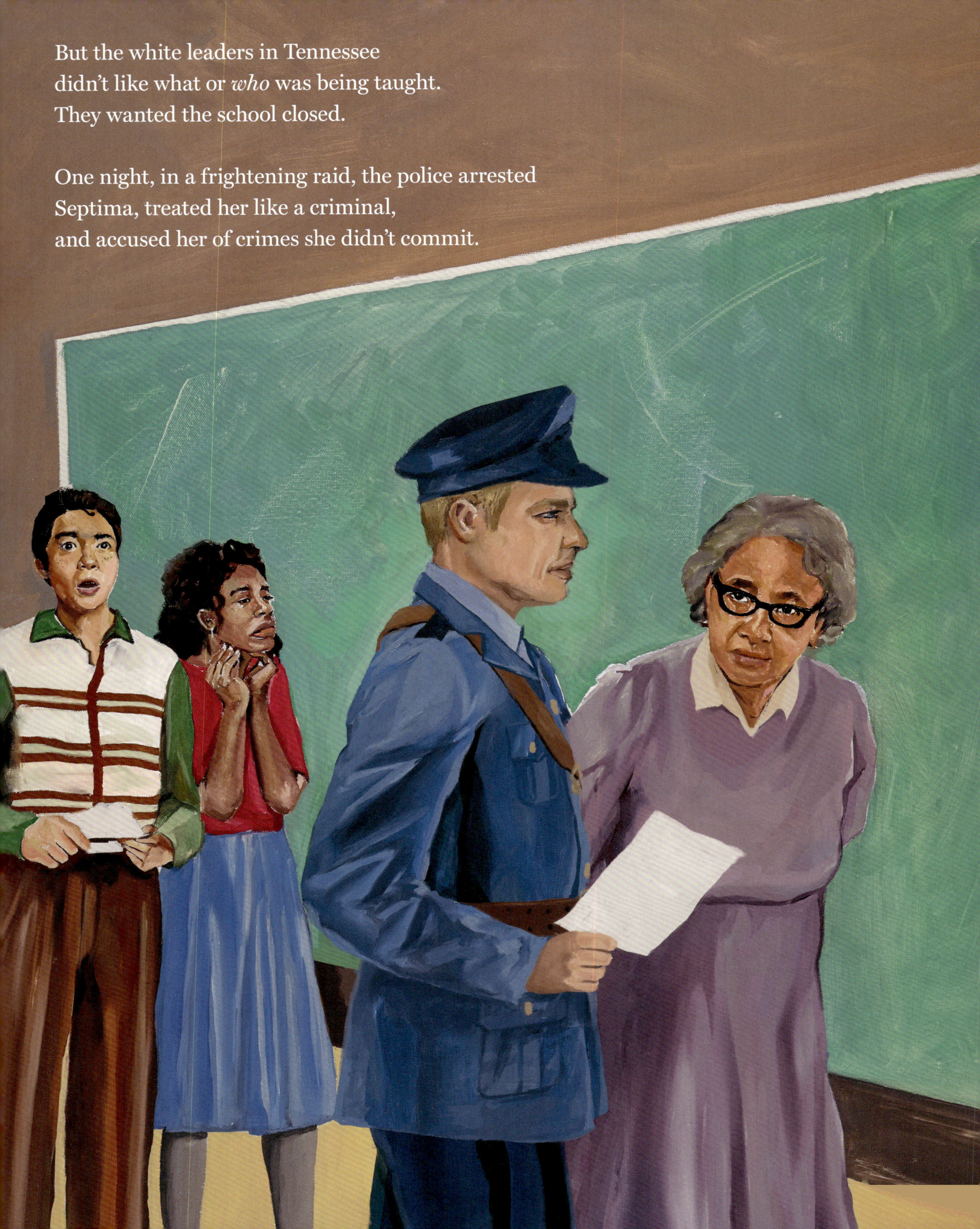

But the white leaders in Tennessee
didn't like what or *who* was being taught.
They wanted the school closed.

One night, in a frightening raid, the police arrested
Septima, treated her like a criminal,
and accused her of crimes she didn't commit.

She sang one of her favorite songs during the ride to the police station—
practicing the nonviolent resistance she taught.
Peace and strength, her parents still whispered in her heart.
That night in jail, Septima felt her tiredness
like a heavy blanket around her shoulders.
She'd been fighting so hard for so long.
Part of her wanted to quit—
get a quiet teaching job and plan her retirement.

But that's *not* what she did.

Ain't gonna let
no jail cell
turn me 'round . . .

Dr. King asked her to lead a new kind of army—
a legion of teachers and voters!

He knew Septima could *always* find a way.

In back rooms and curtained church meetinghouses,
Septima led a quiet revolution,
teaching out of the public eye.

She taught thousands of teachers,
and together, they taught hundreds of thousands of
adult students.

By 1969 Septima's schools had helped
seven hundred thousand Black citizens become legal voters.

Voters who could *be the change.*

I'm gonna keep on a-walkin',
keep on a-talkin',
marchin' up to
freedom land.

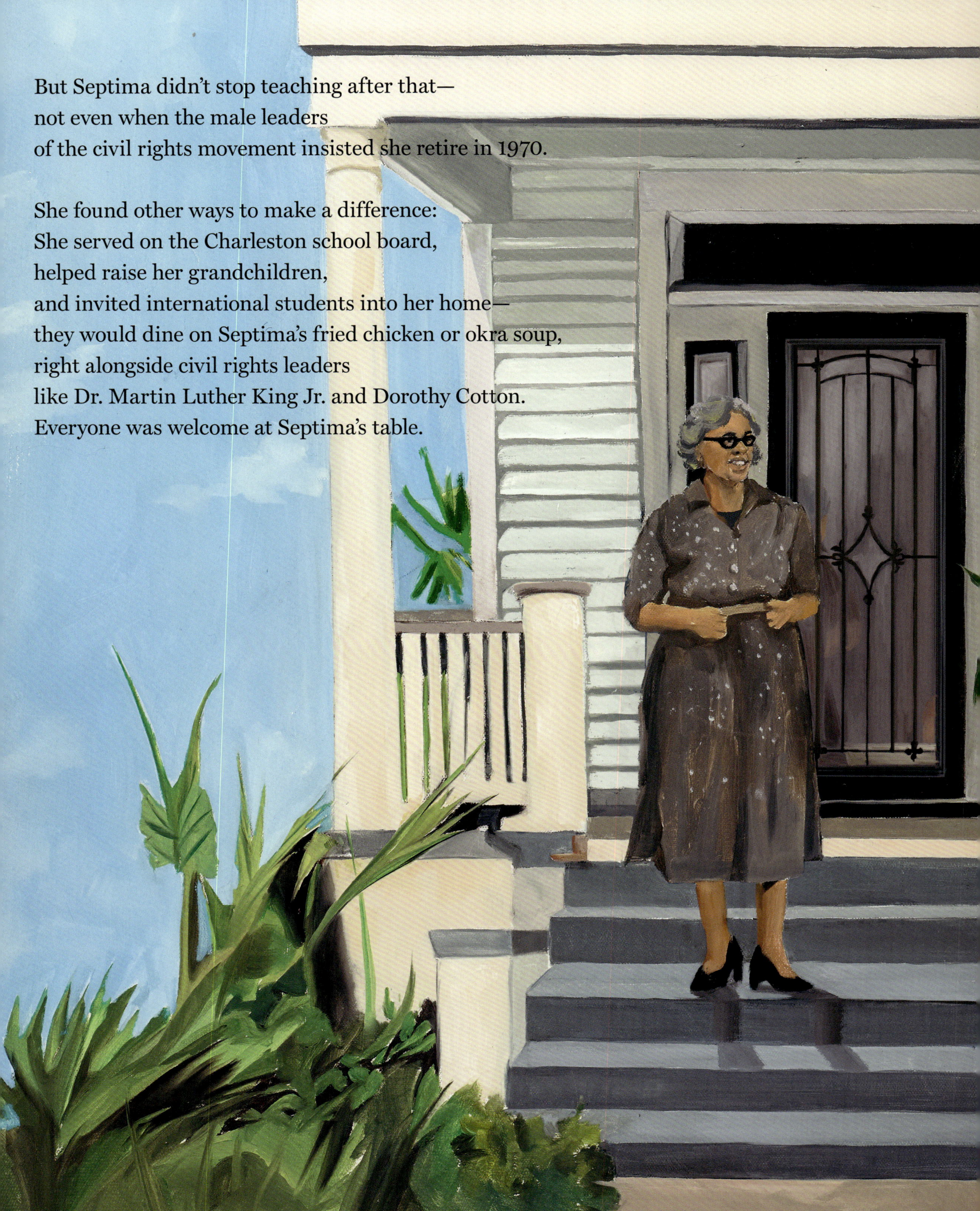

But Septima didn't stop teaching after that—
not even when the male leaders
of the civil rights movement insisted she retire in 1970.

She found other ways to make a difference:
She served on the Charleston school board,
helped raise her grandchildren,
and invited international students into her home—
they would dine on Septima's fried chicken or okra soup,
right alongside civil rights leaders
like Dr. Martin Luther King Jr. and Dorothy Cotton.
Everyone was welcome at Septima's table.

Septima knew—
she *believed*—
that each person was worthy,
and each person deserved
to be heard
to be seen
to be educated.

Because sometimes,
one person
one teacher
and even one VOTE
can make all the difference.

Septima Clark was:
Born poor.
Born Black.
Born a girl.

But she kept teaching and fighting—
making a way where there often seemed to be none.
With peace and strength, hand in hand,
she led her students one step closer to freedom land.

Photo courtesy of Yvonne Clark-Rhines

Authors' Notes

Yvonne Clark-Rhines

Septima is important in many ways. First and foremost, she was a model of what happens when Black people work together with other Black people for the purpose of uplifting us all. She truly was an "each one teach one" living example. Her story of growing up in the time that she did and accomplishing all the many important things that she had is one of perseverance, tenacity, strength, and an attitude of service for her people. There are countless traits of Septima's that should be admired and many triumphs for Black people that will never be forgotten.

Septima was more than a grandmother to me. I was my mother's only girl. On her dying bed, she asked, and Septima answered. Septima became my mother, raising me from the age of five. That's when she became Mama Seppie, or just Mama. She was a loving, strong, giving woman to all who knew her. To this day, I break down in tears attempting to talk about her and what she meant to me. She stepped in again in her senior years to take care of my daughter over summer vacations when I became a single parent. Mama Seppie had the strength of a lion and the heart of an angel.

Mama Seppie is the embodiment of Black Girl (Woman) Magic.

Monica Clark-Robinson

In 1964 Dr. Martin Luther King Jr. traveled to Norway to receive his Nobel Peace Prize. Other than his family, there was just one person he wanted by his side: Septima Poinsette Clark. He told her the Nobel was just as much hers as it was his, and he insisted she accompany him. He called her the Mother of the Movement. Others have called her the Queen Mother or the Grandmother of the Movement. Yet her name isn't often heard, and her story isn't often told.

Looking at the civil rights movement through the lens of the women who were involved tells a very different story from the typical narrative, especially focusing on strong leaders like Septima, Fannie Lou Hamer, Diane Nash, and Dorothy Cotton. Septima herself was bothered by the prejudice she saw against women in the civil rights movement and believed their contributions to be overlooked. She said, "I think the civil rights movement would never have taken off if some women hadn't started to speak up."

Anyone who spent even a little time with Septima came away a better person. Many civil rights leaders were taught by Septima. Even Rosa Parks attended a class! As Rosa watched Ms. Clark, she thought, *If only I could catch some of her spirit . . .*

Three months later, Rosa refused to give up her seat for a white passenger on a bus in Alabama.

In her quiet, determined way, Septima changed the world.

Timeline

May 3, 1898 Septima Poinsette Clark is born in Charleston, South Carolina.

1914 Black teachers begin to be hired to teach in Black schools in Charleston.

1916 Septima graduates from the Avery Normal Institute, the first free secondary school for Blacks.

1916–1919 Teaches at the Promise Land School, an all-Black school on Johns Island

1919 Begins teaching sixth grade at the Avery Normal Institute

Joins the NAACP, the National Association for the Advancement of Colored People

1920 Black principals are permitted in Black schools in Charleston after Septima and her students get ten thousand signatures in one day on a petition to change the "white principals only" rule.

Septima marries Nerie David Clark on May 5.

1921 Septima's daughter, Victoria, is born but dies before she's a month old.

1924 Septima's son, Nerie David Jr., is born.

1925 Septima's husband, Nerie David Clark, dies of kidney failure.

1929 Septima moves to Columbia, South Carolina, and takes a teaching position at Booker T. Washington School.

1942 Receives a bachelor's degree from Benedict College in Columbia

1945 Works with Thurgood Marshall on a court case regarding equal pay for Black and white teachers

1946 Receives a master's degree from Hampton Institute in Hampton, Virginia

1954 Segregation in schools is ruled unconstitutional by the US Supreme Court.

1956 Septima becomes the vice president of the Charleston branch of the NAACP.

The South Carolina legislature passes a law banning state and city employees from holding membership in civil rights organizations. Septima refuses to leave the NAACP, so her teaching position is not renewed.

Septima is hired as the director of workshops at Highlander Folk School in Tennessee, an interracial social justice leadership school for adults, where she begins holding literacy, citizenship, and leadership workshops.

1957 With the help of civil rights activist Esau Jenkins and Highlander Folk School, Septima and her cousin Bernice Robinson create the first "citizenship school" on Johns Island.

1959 Septima is arrested on false charges while teaching at Highlander.

1961 Highlander Folk School is forced to close by the state of Tennessee.

Dr. Martin Luther King Jr. invites Septima to move her citizenship school model to the Southern Christian Leadership Conference. She is the first woman to serve on the organization's board.

1962 Septima publishes her first autobiography, *Echo in My Soul.*

1963 Marches and protests against segregation break out across the South. Dr. King spends eleven days in a Birmingham jail.

Dr. King gives his "I Have a Dream" speech during the March on Washington for Jobs and Freedom on August 28.

President John F. Kennedy is assassinated in Dallas on November 22.

1964 Septima accompanies Dr. King, at his request, when he receives his Nobel Peace Prize in Oslo, Norway.

1968 Dr. Martin Luther King Jr. is assassinated in Memphis.

1969 By 1969 seven hundred thousand Black Americans become citizens, largely thanks to Septima's citizenship schools.

1970 Septima receives the Martin Luther King Jr. Award for Great Service to Humanity from the Southern Christian Leadership Conference.

1972 Elected to the Charleston County School Board and is its first Black female member. She serves two terms.

1979 Receives the Living Legacy Award from President Jimmy Carter

1987 Septima's second autobiography, *Ready from Within*, wins the American Book Award.

December 15, 1987 Septima Poinsette Clark dies on Johns Island, surrounded by family.

Quotes by Septima Poinsette Clark

"I have great belief in the fact that whenever there is chaos, it creates wonderful thinking. I consider chaos a gift."

"The only thing that's really worthwhile is change. It's coming."

"Continued learning is the basis for being richly alive."

"I want people to see children as human beings and not to think of the money that it costs nor to think of the amount of time that it will take, but to think of the lives that can be developed into Americans who will redeem the soul of America and will really make America a great country."

"The greatest evil in our country today is not racism, but ignorance. I believe unconditionally in the ability of people to respond when they are told the truth. We need to be taught to study rather than believe, to inquire rather than to affirm."